For my parents.
And a big thanks to Vicky,
for always listening to my stories,
Kayt, Hannah and Jodie.

Jam and Jelly would like
to thank Alice.

E.E.

First published 2011 by Macmillan Children's Books
an imprint of Pan Macmillan.
20 New Wharf Road, London N1 9RR
Associated companies throughout the world
www.panmacmillan.com
ISBN: 978-0-230-74455-4 (HB)
ISBN: 978-0-230-75068-5 (PB)
Text and illustrations copyright © Elissa Elwick 2011
Moral rights asserted.

3 5 7 9 8 6 4
A CIP catalogue record
for this book is available
from the British Library.
Printed in China.

Elissa Elwick

The PRINCESS
and the
SLEEP STEALER

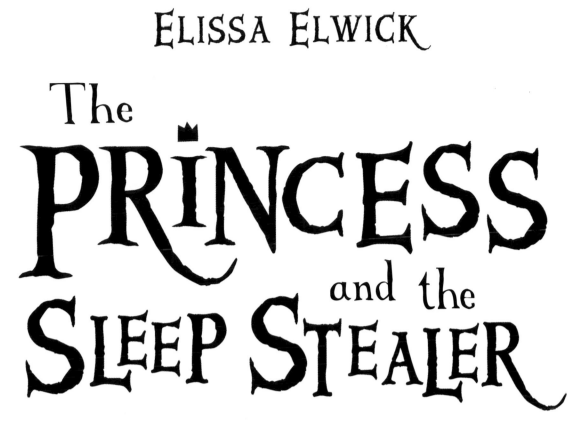

MACMILLAN CHILDREN'S BOOKS

Our story begins in the little town
of Papier, on the top of a hill,
in a castle made of stone.

Inside the castle lives a princess called Luna
and her two Bobwobs, Jam and Jelly.

Princess Luna is the Sleep Keeper
of the town of Papier – a very important job!

Every night, as the castle clock strikes
bedtime, she sprinkles sleepy dust
out of her bedroom window, sending
everyone fast asleep until morning.

But one night, when Princess Luna went to fetch her bag of sleepy dust, it was GONE!

"Oh no," she cried. "The naughty little Sleep Stealer must have taken it. We must get it back before bedtime or no one will be able to sleep!"

"Bobbob," said the Bobwobs, excitedly. They had spotted a trail of pirate treasure leading out of the door.

"Come on!" said Princess Luna.
"There's no time to lose."

Down,

down,

down
they went,

into
the depths
of the castle.

Finally they reached a door in the darkest corner of the dungeon.

Princess Luna opened it . . .

. . . and she and the Bobwobs stepped into a strange new world.

"Welcome to the Land of the Three Zees," yawned three funny-looking creatures. "We're Zim, Zam and Zoo. How do you do?"

Princess Luna told the Three Zees all about the missing sleepy dust and the trail of pirate treasure.

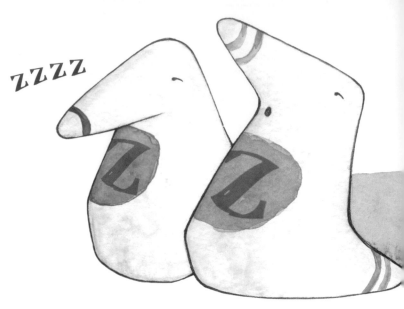

"No sleep? That's terrible!" said Zim, dozily. "Sleeping is what we love best!"

"We saw a little pirate," yawned Zoo. "He went that way." And with that, the Three Zees fell fast asleep.

So off they went, a Princess and her Bobwobs, to find the Sleep Stealer and save bedtime.

They marched over the Sugar Mountains,

between the liquorice trees

and through the boogily whatsits,   until they came to . . .

the shores of the Seven Seas
and a dark and scary
forest, where a gigantic
monster was roaring a
monstrous roar!

Roooaaar!

Jam and Jelly wobbled with
fear as the monster and
its horrible howling
got closer
and closer.

But it wasn't a monster at all!
It was a not-so-scary dragon, and he
was singing a lullaby, very badly!

"Hello," he warbled.
"I'm Dragon Fly. Have you
come to hear me sing?"
Princess Luna giggled.
"No, we're chasing a
sleep-stealing pirate."

"Oh!" Dragon Fly cried. "A pirate
ship has just set sail. We can
catch it if we're quick!"

So Princess Luna, Jam and Jelly climbed
onto Dragon Fly's back and they
soared across the Seven Seas.

It wasn't long before a pirate ship
appeared, bobbing on the water.
It was the Sleep Stealer, and
his fearsome crew!

"Give me my sleepy dust!"
cried Princess Luna.
"If you want it, come and get it!"
shouted the Sleep Stealer.

Dragon Fly swooped onto the
deck and the battle began.

Swords clashed,

Dragon Fly sang as
loudly as he could,

and the Bobwobs
began to climb.

"Bobbobwobbob," they cried. They had spotted the sleepy dust, hidden in the crow's nest!

They sprinkled it down over the Sleep Stealer and his crew . . .

ZZZZ

. . . sending them all fast asleep.

So at one minute to bedtime, and with the sleepy dust safe in her hands, Princess Luna and her friends flew back towards the door that led to the castle.

They tiptoed past the snoozing Three Zees, hugged
Dragon Fly goodbye and ran back through the door.

As the clock began to chime,
they raced up, up, up the stairs.

"Just in time," sighed Princess Luna,
and she sprinkled sleepy dust
down onto the town below.
"Sweet dreams," she whispered.

Sweet dreams, Princess Luna.
Sweet dreams, Jam.
Sweet dreams, Jelly.

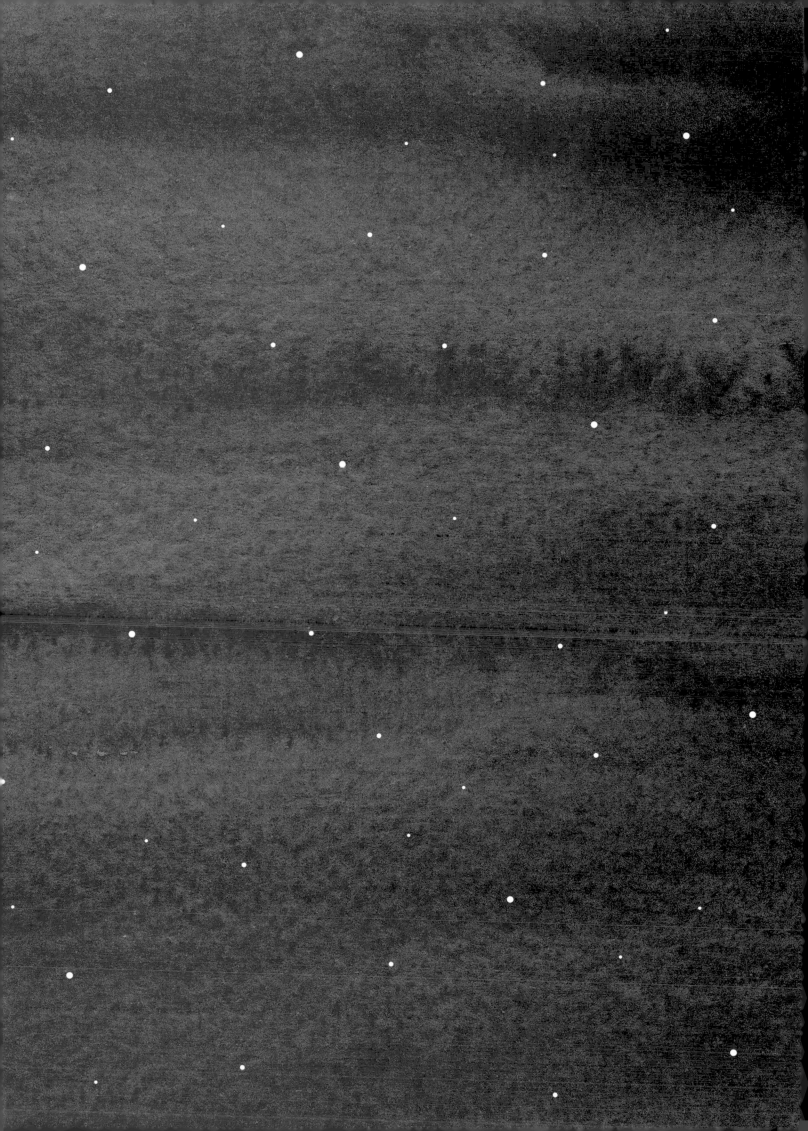